The ALLIGATORS Next Door

Written by Kerry Dancer
Illustrated by her Grandchildren

The Alligators Next Door
Illustrated by Shayne and Zain Garrido
Cover Design by Dwayne Garrido

ACKNOWLEDGEMENT

A wonderful man named Nicholas Amodio inspired this book. I was intrigued while reading an article in my local newspaper about the city trying to force this man to get rid of his pet alligators. I was deeply concerned about the welfare of these animals. I was also disturbed by the thought of Mr. Amodio having to give up pets that he loved with all his heart. Nick hatched these alligators from eggs and has raised them for 30 years.

The Alligators Next Door

Kerry Dancer

NEW BEGINNING

Nick was 10 years old when his parents divorced. Nick didn't have any brothers or sisters. He was an only child. Sometimes an only child will feel lonely and bored, but not Nick. He had 57 pets to keep him company and they were always entertaining. Nick's favorite pets were named Annie and Alex. Annie and Alex were born 2 weeks after Nick's father moved out. Thanks to them, divorce wasn't so sad.

Nick's mother, Jill was a veterinarian and brought new animals home from the hospital every week. These animals needed special care to get well. Some animals stayed for a day or two, but some never left. Nick's dad said he left because Jill cared more about the animals than him. Nick's mom said he left because he fell in love with Barbie. Nick didn't know Barbie and didn't understand why grown-ups got married or divorced.

FIRST DAY OF SPRING

The first day of spring always brought joy to Nick's house. This year was especially warm and sunny. The flowers were in bloom and the air was fresh and smelled of rose gardens. Nick went to work with his mom on Saturday. He loved helping her at the office. Nick, like his mother, loved animals. He felt so proud watching her save lives and nurture sick animals.

A little girl named Amy was in the waiting room crying. She and her mother brought in their dog that had been hit by a car. She was afraid that her dog would die.

Nick put his arms around her and said, "Don't worry little girl, my mom will save your dog." Sure enough, Jill and Amy's mother walked through the examination room's door carrying Amy's dog.

"Amy", Jill said, in a soft and caring voice, "your dog broke his leg so I put a cast around it. You can take him home now. He's going to be fine. I'll remove the cast in 6 weeks."

Amy was so happy as they carried their dog to the car. Nick ran to the side of the office to pick a rose for Amy, but came across a mysterious can next to the rose bush.

Inside the can was dirt and mud. Nestled deep in the mud were 2 large bird eggs. Nick didn't have time to pick roses; the eggs needed urgent attention. He carefully carried the can to the back room.

Jill said, "What are you doing with that smelly old coffee can?" The dirt had a musky, moldy smell to it.

"Someone left it outside Mom", said Nick. "It has some kind of bird eggs in it. Can we take them home, Mom? We only have 30 birds now. I'm tired of watching chickens hatch. I want a new bird. I'm sure Harriet; the hen will sit on them for me. Can we please take them home Mom?"

"I don't recognize the breed Nick. We'll have to look in our bird encyclopedia tonight", said Jill.

Before leaving the office, Nick picked a bunch of red roses for his mother. As they drove home, they didn't notice the musky, moldy smell of the dirt because the fragrant roses filled the car with spring scents.

When they arrived home, Jill took the roses to the kitchen while Nick carried the coffee can to the hen house. He carefully placed it in a corner next to Harriet, the hen. He wasn't sure how to coax Harriet to sit on the eggs. Harriet was an old fat hen who was very bossy. She'd push the other hens out of the way instead of saying excuse me. Harriet wasn't accustomed to sitting on eggs that didn't belong to her. Nick decided to just pick her up and place her gently on top of the can. She immediately jumped off squawking and squawking. Nick persisted in trying 10 times until the exhausted hen finally gave in. Nick felt content seeing Harriet adopt the mystery eggs.

He went in the house to join his mother for dinner. Right after dinner, Nick got ready for bed. He was so anxious to get back to the eggs. He planned on getting up early, before Harriet would get up.

BABIES HATCH

The sun peeked through the window shades, shining in Nick's eyes and awakening him abruptly. He anxiously jumped out of bed, slipped into shoes, and dashed to the hen house. Nick was relieved to find Harriet still on top of the can. Joey, Nick's dog ran into the hen house barking and startled Harriet right off of the can.

"Joey", yelled Nick, "bad dog, what's wrong with you?"

When Joey became quiet, Nick could hear a tap, tap, tapping noise coming from the eggs. He listened intently. It sounded like the eggs were talking to each other. One egg would tap, then the other egg would tap back. I think these birds are about to hatch, Nick thought to himself.

TAP, TAP, TAP,
LET ME OUT.
TAP, TAP, TAP,
LET US OUT.
TAP FOR ME,
TAP FOR YOU,
TAP TOGETHER,
THAT MAKES TWO.

Nick carried a bench and placed it in front of the eggs. He sat there patiently waiting for the eggs to hatch. Nick could hear his mother calling.

"Nick, where are you?" yelled Jill. Joey ran to Jill barking and brought her to Nick.

"What are you doing honey", asked Nick's mom.

"I think the eggs are going to hatch Mom. I don't want to miss it!" replied Nick.

"OK dear, I'll bring your breakfast to you. Would you like orange juice or apple juice?"

"Orange juice please." Nick ate his breakfast, waited, and waited, and still no birds. He decided to take a break. He'd take a quick shower and get dressed. He wouldn't be gone for long. An hour went by and Nick returned to the hen house.

"Oh no!" Nick screamed. The eggs had hatched and he missed it! He also didn't see any baby birds. He didn't see Harriet either. Nick ran around the back yard searching for Harriet and the new babies.

He found Harriet next to the pond squawking louder than he's ever heard her squawk before. The pond was filled with goldfish and 10 turtles. At the other end of the pond, Nick could see something moving.

He ran to the other end and was dumbfounded by his discovery. In the pond, eating goldfish were 2 baby alligators!

"Mom, Mom", Nick cried while running inside the house. "You're not going to believe what kind of eggs we just hatched. They aren't birds at all. They're alligators", Nick exclaimed out of breath.

"Alligators", said Jill. "What are we going to do with alligators?"

"Oh Mom, I've never had a pet alligator. I have to keep them!" begged Nick. Jill didn't know what to say. She had no experience or education on raising reptiles.

"We can't keep them honey. I'll find a local zoo to take them," replied Jill. "No Mom, I'll look on the

Internet and research how to raise alligators. I'll find out everything we need to know and I will take care of them. Please don't take them away from me.", pleaded Nick.

"Well, you can keep them for 30 days and I'll reevaluate the situation then", answered Jill.

Nick gave his mom a big hug and thanked her. He went to the garage and found a big wooden crate to put the alligators in. He filled it with grass and dirt. He took the alligators to his bedroom and logged onto his computer. He found a lot of valuable information about alligators and found a pet store that specialized in reptiles. He phoned the store and spoke to a man named William. William said he knew a lot about alligators. He told Nick to bring the alligators to the store and he would be happy to help him.

The next day, Nick, his mom, and the alligators took a trip to the reptile store and met William. William examined the alligators and said, "They look healthy and you've got 1 of each; 1 boy and 1 girl. Here's a 50-gallon aquarium. Fill it with grass and mud. Place a water dish in the corner. Keep them in this until they outgrow it. When they outgrow this container, they are ready for the outdoors. Then you'll have to build a proper pen to keep them in. For the first 6 months feed them goldfish and crickets twice a day.

When they reach 6 months, add raw chicken with bones. At 1 year, feed them only chicken."

Jill purchased the aquarium, water dish, a book about alligators, and 100 live crickets. On the way home, Nick and his mom played the name game. What to name the alligators game. Nick insisted that the names begin with an "A" like Alligator.

They called names out loud: "Allen, Adam, Alexander, Alex, Andy, and Anthony for the boys names. Then, "Amanda, Allison, Ann, Annie, Angela, and Antonia" for the girls names. They said them out loud over and over again until they reached their final decision.

The alligators now had names: Annie and Alex. When they got home, Nick prepared their new aquarium.

During the next few months, Nick's chores increased. He didn't realize how much more work 2 more pets would create. In the morning before school, Nick spent an hour or more feeding all the animals. When he came home from school he spent 2 hours cleaning up the yard, cages, and hen house along with feeding all the animals again.

Other kids played sports, went to movies, played computer games, and watched television. Not Nick; he had too much work to do. He never complained. Nick felt so fortunate to experience raising so many types of animals. He learned a lot of valuable lessons from them. Animals teach people about survival and about loving all of God's creatures.

Baby alligators are very unusual and fascinating pets. They didn't fetch sticks or balls, they didn't sit or roll over, but they loved to play chase.

Nick would go up to Alex and yell, "chase me, chase me". Nick would start running and Alex would follow right behind him. They would chase each other until Nick was exhausted.

Annie and Alex would then jump in the pond to cool off. Annie often hitched a ride on one of the turtle's backs. The turtle would give her a ride all around the pond.

ONE YEAR LATER

The first year went by so fast. Annie and Alex were now 1 year old and living in the backyard with all of the other animals. They had adapted really well. Nick and Jill became very knowledgeable about alligators during the past year and truly loved Annie and Alex.

Nick didn't want to go to school for fear that he'd miss something exciting. Nick's mother reminded him every day that school was too important to miss; even with the valuable education he was gaining from the alligators.

Jill was often tempted to stay home with Annie and Alex and miss work, but she realized it was her responsibility to go to work every day and take care of all the animals that needed her. In the past 20 years, Jill had only missed work 3 times when she was really sick.

Besides, Annie and Alex were quite content during the day without Nick and Jill.

The alligators had very unique personalities and interesting habits. As soon as the sun would rise, Alex would slip into the pond and slowly glide from one end to the other. He would blow bubbles whenever he approached a turtle or any of the animals. It seemed like blowing bubbles was his way of saying Good morning, isn't it a beautiful day. After cruising back and forth several times, he would park himself in a particular spot and lay completely still for hours.

Whenever Alex would finish a meal, he would lay at the side of the embankment on the shady side of the pond and think about how lucky he was to have such a wonderful family. This is the spot where he always slept.

Annie was adventurous and loved to explore. Throughout the day, she would wander from one corner of the yard to the other. She left no ground untouched. Annie followed a routine path paved with scheduled stops along the way. Annie slept close to the driveway and would begin her day lying in a sunny spot in the middle of the driveway. Her routine path always followed the sun. One of her first stops in the morning was on the front porch.

Nick always fed Annie on the front porch. He called it the dining quarters for the princess. After breakfast, Annie would continue on her path through the yard, stopping along the way to smell the flowers, greeting Alex, the turtles, the chickens, and any animals that crossed her path. Annie loved to socialize.

Late afternoon, she would slide into the pond. Annie liked to wait until the water was really warm before swimming. Alex would always join Annie and they would swim together for hours. Nick loved watching Annie and Alex swim together in the pond. He was fascinated by the way they played together. Alex would be relaxing in the water when he would hear Annie calling him.

Annie would be at the opposite side of the pond making soft hissing sounds. Alex could hear her from anywhere in the yard, even from under water.

Alligators have excellent hearing. When they swim under water their movable flaps cover their ears. These flaps prevent water from getting in the ear canal. When Alex would hear Annie's call, he would dive under water and sneak up on her. He would obviously startle her because she would let out this loud bellowing noise.

Annie and Alex took turns swimming from one end of the pond to the other. They continually made hissing sounds while they played. These sounds were their way of communicating. The loud bellowing noises were their method of shouting. Sometimes it sounded like they were arguing. Nick always wondered what they were saying to each other. Their language was very intriguing to Nick.

Annie and Alex displayed a unique style of movement. Nick was often amused watching them roam. They were graceful and smooth in the water, but usually clumsy and slow on land. The only time they weren't clumsy and slow on land was when they were in a hurry. Any sense of urgency would accelerate the speed of their movement.

One day Alex was exceptionally hungry. His keen sense of smell told him that dinner was on its way. He dashed down the hill to the porch in 2 minutes flat. His maneuver was so swift; he appeared to be flying.

Annie always got out of the pond first and would proceed to her favorite sunbathing spot on the wooden bridge. Jill called it Annie's bridge. Alex always stayed in the pond until the dinner bell rang.

When dinner was ready, Nick rang a big brass bell. It rang so loud with a clang, clang, clang. Annie and Alex would both join Nick on the front porch for dinner. On warm summer nights, Nick and his mom would eat dinner on the porch with Annie and Alex. They would eat at the patio table.

There would be a slight breeze, carrying summer scents of roses, tulips, daffodils, orange blossoms, and the occasional neighborhood barbecue. It was a pleasant dining experience for all. Nick would bring Joey's dog dish onto the porch also. It was not the traditional American family dinner.

At night, Annie slept with Bubba and Lulu; the 200-pound pot bellied pigs. She liked to sleep right in between the two pigs to keep warm. They slept under a canopy of eucalyptus trees. Their shelter was adjacent to the driveway.

One Thursday evening, Nick was doing homework when his mom came home with 2 baby raccoons. She named them Randy and Ricky. Their mother died and they were too young to feed themselves. They needed to be bottle fed. Nick quickly volunteered to feed them. Raccoons never leave their mothers' side and because Nick fed them every day, they believed he was their mother. They followed him everywhere he went, even to school.

In the morning, Nick would place his backpack over his shoulders not realizing that Randy had climbed inside. Ricky would wait by the front door and follow so close to Nick that Nick couldn't see him. While school was in session, Randy and Ricky would sleep under Nick's desk.

Many of Nick's friends came to visit Annie and Alex on a regular basis. Most of them lived in Nick's neighborhood and several were friends from school.

Nick's best friend was a girl named Lorraine. She was in Nick's class. She didn't have any pets at her house, so she loved going to Nick's house. She said it was more fun than the zoo. Lorraine liked to help Nick after school. She helped him with cleaning the yard and feeding the animals. Nick appreciated Lorraine's help because the chores didn't take so long. On the days Lorraine helped there was an extra hour to either watch TV or play games. Nick's mom would serve special home baked chocolate chip cookies and milk on these days.

FIVE YEARS LATER

How many 16-year-old boys have pets that are 8 feet long and weigh 400 pounds? Nick was a very fortunate teenager. His friends loved going to his house to visit Annie and Alex. Most of the kids in the neighborhood would visit at least twice a week. Some parents were afraid to let their small children visit for fear they'd be eaten by alligators.

Nick couldn't understand why anyone would be afraid of Annie or Alex. In 6 years, they never showed any type of aggressive behavior. They got along with all animals and people. They were actually the tamest of all Nick's pets. His dog barked and growled, the turtles snapped, raccoons would bite, but Annie and Alex were always peaceful, gentle, and kind.

One Saturday afternoon, Nick was in the backyard mowing the lawn. He had just shut off the mower when he was startled by a loud noise. It sounded like a speeding wave runner splashing on the ocean. Nick ran to the pond and saw Alex excitedly doing the "headslap". The "headslap" is a motion alligators do by slamming their head onto the water over and over again to get another alligator's attention.

Alex wasn't trying to get another alligator's attention. He was calling Nick to alert him to an emergency situation. Nick looked all around the yard near Alex until he spotted a little baby bird that had fallen out of its nest. Nick picked up the baby bird and placed it back in the nest, which was in the tree next to the pond. Alex immediately became quiet. Nick got down on his knees, called Alex over to him, and gave him a big hug.

Later that evening, Nick noticed the full moon. He was just about to watch his favorite television show when he heard tires and brakes screeching. Seconds later he heard a loud crash. Nick and his mother both ran outside to see what happened. A big car had a streetlight pole wrapped around it.

Nick ran in the house and dialed 911. Moments later, 2 Policemen, 2 Firemen, and 1 ambulance arrived at the scene. An old man was trapped inside and appeared to be unconscious. Neither the Policemen nor the Firemen were able to get the car doors open.

One Fireman said he would call in a request for "The Jaws of Life" equipment. He said it might take 20 minutes to arrive and was worried that it could be too late.

When Nick heard the Fireman say "The Jaws of Life" he immediately had a brilliant idea. Alligators have such strong jaws that they can crush more than 10 tons of steel.

Nick ran to the back yard and commanded Alex to come to him. Alex detected the urgent tone in Nick's voice and responded quickly.

Alex followed Nick to the car and the Policemen and the Firemen jumped back 5 feet frightened.

Nick said, "Don't be afraid, Alex will snap that pole in half. His jaws are just as powerful as "The Jaws of Life." It's a good thing that alligators are nocturnal because with the streetlight down it was very dark.

Nick instructed Alex to the exact place on the pole where he wanted him to bite.

"OK Alex, bite", he yelled, "bite Alex bite."

Alex opened his mouth as wide as he could and fiercely snapped the pole in half.

"Good boy", shouted Nick, "Good boy."

The Firemen were able to move the pole, open the door, and pull the man out of the car. They laid him on a stretcher and administered CPR.

The old man regained consciousness and everyone took turns petting and hugging Alex. The ambulance drove the man to the nearest hospital.

Jill, Nick, and Alex went back to their activities. What a day this had been.

A few weeks later on a Sunday morning, Nick went into the kitchen and found the room flooded. He called for his mother who screamed as she entered the kitchen.

"Nick", said his Mom, "I have to go to work for an emergency surgery. Please call a plumber and have them come out immediately. Explain to the plumber that this has happened at least 2 other times and we were told that the pipes in the backyard need routine cleaning."

When the plumber arrived, Nick was in the middle of cooking pancakes for breakfast. He showed the man to the back door and explained to him what needed to be done. Nick finished cooking his pancakes, turned on the television and began eating.

All of a sudden he remembered that he forgot to tell the plumber about the alligators. He peeked out the kitchen window first to see if everything was all right. The man looked frozen staring at Annie. He looked confused and petrified. He obviously couldn't tell if she was real or fake.

Suddenly the man bent over and grabbed Annie as if he was going to pick her up to move her out of his way. At that moment Annie turned her head up and looked at him.

The plumber was so startled he couldn't move and his face turned as white as a ghost. Nick ran outside apologizing for the situation and assuring him that Annie would not hurt him.

Nick told Annie to move to the other side of the yard and there she went obediently. The man said he needed a glass of water and was feeling faint.

Nick brought a tall glass of ice water and suggested that he sit down and rest for a while. About 10 minutes later the man regained his composure and unclogged the drains.

When Nick told his mom what had happened, they both laughed hysterically.

CITY HALL

Jill checked the mail one summer afternoon. She received a letter from the City Hall. They were informing her that under new jurisdiction laws the alligators could not live in this city. The city had become incorporated and the council had voted on new animal licensing rules. The letter also stated that several neighbors had complained. Some neighbors complained that the birds were too noisy and others complained that they did not feel safe with wild alligators in their neighborhood. Jill showed the letter to Nick who was now 18 years old.

Nick yelled, "Annie and Alex are not wild animals and they would never hurt anyone."

"I know honey, I'll call a lawyer friend of mine and find out what our legal rights are", said Jill.

During the next month, Jill consulted with a lawyer, prepared her case, and met with neighbors and friends. June 18 arrived, the day of the City Council meeting. Nick and his mom were both very nervous about the outcome of the meeting. What would they do if they had to move Annie and Alex?

The meeting began at 7:00 p.m. sharp and the room was filled with people. There were 2 television cameras with eyewitness reporters. First the Council spokesperson read the complaints and request to move the alligators. Jill was asked to speak next. Nick stood by her side. She spoke calmly eventhough she was nervous inside.

"My son, Nick brought 2 eggs home 8 years ago believing they were bird eggs. When they hatched we were amazed to find out that they were baby alligators. We have raised them with many different animals and they are by far the tamest pets we've ever had. They have never displayed aggressive or threatening behavior. Our neighbors bring their children over to visit Annie and Alex. I've acquired every permit and license that the county has requested of me. I built a safe environment for the animals and the neighborhood", commented Jill.

The next speaker was a neighbor named Tom who was an architectural engineer.

"The alligators next door pose no threat to our quiet neighborhood. I've lived next door for 10 years. I remember the day the alligators hatched. My 2 sons were really excited.

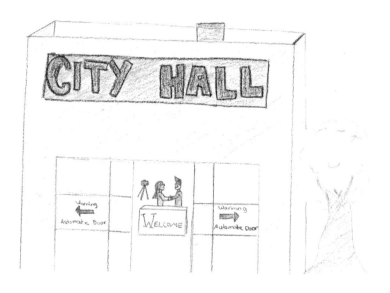

Since then the boys and I have visited Annie and Alex at least twice a week for the last 8 years. I helped build the alligator pen and hired the best inspector I knew to conduct the safety inspection.

That yard is like Fort Knox. Jill is a great veterinarian and loves all animals. All of her pets are properly cared for. She is always helping neighbors with their pets. Jill takes pride in sharing her animals with guests. She always says, this is not just for my enjoyment, but for all to enjoy. She welcomes visitors daily".

During the 3-hour meeting, over 40 people, mostly neighbors, spoke on behalf of keeping the alligators. Only 2 people spoke against them. At 10:00 p.m., the announcement was made. The alligators can stay providing requested improvements are completed by stated due dates. The crowd cheered while Nick and Jill were interviewed by reporters.

THE END

"THE ALLIGATORS NEXT DOOR" is a very enchanting children's book. I am flattered and honored to have inspired and contributed to this book.

I would like to clarify that even though this book was based on true stories; it is not a true story.

I would like to caution all readers about safety with alligators. It is true that my pet alligators, Bonnie and Clyde are tame and safe to pet.

However, this is not true of alligators in the wild or at zoos. I also cannot speak of any other pet alligators that people have.

Please do not get close to or attempt to pet an alligator that you don't know for sure is safe.

Nicholas Amodio

Made in the USA
Middletown, DE
28 May 2015